NORA
A NEANDERTHAL GIRL

Author's Note: Although based on anthropological evidence from Neanderthal sites, *Nora, a Neanderthal girl* is a work of fiction. The characters and events are a product of the author's imagination.

Copyright © 2022 Mary A. Graves

The author gives appropriate credit to photos sourced from Wikimedia Commons. For the book's interior design, decorative art is sourced from ©AFstudio57, ©Amran Gany, and ©Perfectorius through a fee paid to Shutterstock by Karina Granda.

All rights reserved. This book and any portion thereof may not be reproduced or used in any manner whatsoever without the written permission of the author except for the use of brief quotations in a book review.

ISBN 978-0-578-39716-0 (ebook)
ISBN 979-8-9862889-0-1 (paperback)

Illustrations by Isabel Arné
Cover and interior design by Karina Granda

First Printing 2022

NORA
A NEANDERTHAL GIRL

By Mary A. Graves

*I dedicate this book to my brother, Tom.
He bikes, he gardens, he cooks, he built his house, he
is always reading something interesting. He hardly
ever uses his car; he takes buses and trains. He grows
a lot of the food that he eats in his garden. He is the
most amazing person I have ever met!*

INTRODUCTION

TODAY, HUMANS ARE THE ONLY HOMININS who live on planet Earth. A long time ago, humans lived next to other hominins like Neanderthals. About 20,000 years ago, the last Neanderthal died, and Neanderthals became extinct. The only hominins left were the humans.

This is a story about a Neanderthal girl named Nora and her cousin Runi. They lived more than 20,000 years ago in a cave with their families and friends.

Photo credit: Mary A. Graves (2018), Shanidar Cave

Shanidar Cave, Iraq

This photo shows the entrance to Shanidar Cave in Iraq. Ralph Solecki, an anthropologist from Columbia University, and his team began digging in the cave in 1951. They discovered the skeletons of 10 Neanderthal men, women, and children. These skeletons are evidence that Neanderthals lived in Shanidar Cave. Most of what we know about Neanderthals is from evidence found in caves like this one. Many Neanderthal children, like Nora and Runi in this story, would have lived in a cave like Shanidar Cave. Today, anthropologist Emma Pomeroy and her team from Cambridge University continue to find exciting new evidence about Neanderthals in Shanidar Cave.

CHAPTER ONE

NORA FEELS A SOFT BREEZE ON HER FACE. She yawns, shivers, then snuggles down under the animal skins covering her. She sighs softly, opens her eyes, and looks up. Her eyes follow the sunlight slowly moving across the ceiling of the cave. She hears her mom adding wood to the fireplace nearby. Suddenly, Nora remembers that today is the day her mom told her she could go hunting with her cousin Runi. Now Nora is wide awake. She quickly jumps out of bed and slips on her deerskin dress before walking over to the fire, where her mom is sitting.

"Here, have these," her mom says, handing her some nuts. Nora takes the nuts and begins cracking one open. After eating a few of them, Nora looks at her mom and says, "This is one of my favorite breakfasts."

"I know," her mom replies.

Then Nora says, "Mom, remember you said that Runi and I can go hunting today? You said we couldn't go on the grown-up deer hunt but we could have our own rabbit hunt."

"Yes, you and Runi will have your hunt today," replies her mom. "But I want you to slow down and finish eating before you run off."

Just then, Runi walks from the other side of the cave, where his family sleeps, to the fireplace. He says good morning to Nora and her mom. He sits down next to Nora.

"Are you excited?" he asks.

"Yes! But I need to sharpen my spear," says Nora.

"I do too," he replies.

Nora's mom looks at the two of them. "Now, hunting is a skill that takes a lot of practice. Work together as a team and you can bring down even big animals. Here are a few things I want you to remember. I don't want the two of you to go too far from our cave. Stay on this side of the mountain. Bring along a pouch for food. If you find

anything to add to dinner tonight, you can put it in the pouch. Besides hunting, you might have time to find some fruit or nuts."

"Sure, Mom, we'll be out front for a while sharpening our spears, then we'll move to the brush and trees below," replies Nora. "We might be at the bottom of the mountain or near the river, but we'll always be where we can see our cave. We'll keep our spears close. And if we find any berries, we'll bring some home."

Holding their spears, Nora and Runi walk outside their cave into the sunshine.

"Let's sit on that boulder over there," suggests Nora. Runi follows Nora to some nearby boulders.

Nora sits down and begins running her hand up and down the side of her spear looking for bumps. She examines each bump closely and picks off tiny pieces of wood with her fingers. She takes out her flaked stone tool that she uses for scraping. She holds it in her hand with the sharp side pointing outward. She scrapes down the side of her spear until it is smooth. Then she carefully files the tip of her spear until it comes to a sharp point. She blows the dust off the tip and then puts her flaked stone tool away. She is ready.

Nora looks over at Runi, who is still working on his spear. "I hope we have a good hunt and bring something back," she says. "It's starting to get cooler at night. In the winter, finding food is harder. So, every time I go out, I want to be a stronger tracker and hunter."

"Well," Runi replies, "I want to really improve throwing my spear because I miss my target a lot. I just want to be more accurate."

"Is hunting more important to you than tracking?" Nora asks.

"A long time ago," Runi replies, "during a hunt, my grandpa's arm was trampled by a cave bear, and when he fell, he hurt his legs too. If the hunters had thrown their spears more accurately, the cave bear would have gone down right away and no one would have been hurt."

"That's true," says Nora. "Accuracy matters. But if you can't find the animals, you can't hunt them."

"You've been on more rabbit hunts and killed more rabbits than I have," Runi replies. "Right now, I'm worried about my accuracy. But by remembering where the rabbits are now, we have a better chance of finding where they live in the winter."

"Yes," Nora says, "and the snow will help us see their footprints."

While Nora waits for Runi to finish, she watches a bird fly down and nibble on some flowers. Then she looks out in the far distance where the river curls around a group of trees. "I'm done," says Runi after a while. They walk slowly down the hill toward a field with some bushes and tree stumps where they have seen rabbits before.

Photo credit: Geni (2018), Clacton Spear, License GFDL

The earliest known wooden spear point

This is the tip of the earliest known wooden spear. It was discovered in Clacton-on-Sea, England. It is 420,000 years old and is made of yew wood. It is evidence that hunting was important during the time of the Neanderthals. This wooden spear point would have been made by scraping the wood with a sharp stone tool. In this story, Nora and Runi are throwing small spears because they are hunting rabbits. But adult Neanderthals would have used bigger and stronger spears that could take down large animals.

CHAPTER TWO

AS NORA AND RUNI APPROACH THE FIELD, they smell the fresh scent of trees and shrubs. Insects are buzzing and birds are chirping. It's late summer and warm, but the cool breeze hints that autumn is around the corner.

Nora and Runi become silent and begin to look for rabbits. Slowly, Nora separates from Runi until they are about eight paces apart. They can see each other out of the corners of their eyes. Both become vigilant and look around for any movement, noise, or sign of rabbits. They scan the ground and their surroundings. They look for footprints, broken twigs, and even rabbit poop. They stay alert for any sign that a rabbit might have been there. Slowly they move forward at the same pace. It is very peaceful. Then Nora sees something move near a bush, and she signals to Runi. They lock eyes and become perfectly still. The sun is shining. Nora can feel the heat and the breeze on her face. After waiting a while and seeing no more movement, the two children gently and quietly walk forward again. They continue stopping and starting as they move through the field and some brush.

And then, after an hour or so, Runi stops. Nora follows his example and looks where he is looking, which is a tree stump near a bush. They wait again in perfect silence. Suddenly, a rabbit bolts toward the bush. Nora races after it, with Runi right behind her. During the split second when the rabbit turns, Nora lunges forward. She throws her spear directly at the rabbit. The rabbit dodges the spear and bounds off.

"So close!" shouts Runi. "You barely missed it."

Nora goes up to the area near the bush

and picks up her spear. She shrugs her shoulders and says, "It doesn't matter if I miss by a lot or by a little—it's still a miss."

The children continue looking for rabbits. Suddenly, Runi hears a rustle behind some bushes. He peers over the bushes and sees a single rabbit between two trees. He signals to Nora. She signals back that she sees the rabbit. The rabbit hears Runi and Nora moving. It races away behind one of the trees.

After hunting for a couple of hours, Nora looks over at Runi and says, "I'm getting hungry. What about you?"

"Kind of. Do you want to eat some berries from the bushes near the river?" asks Runi.

"Yes. It's not too far, and we can have a drink too," Nora replies.

Nora and Runi walk down the hill toward a patch of berry bushes. They begin picking berries. They make two piles of berries on top of a flat boulder. They sit on the boulder and carefully put the berries from one pile into the pouch. Then they slowly eat the berries from the other pile. They lie flat on the boulder and take a rest in the sun. The heat rising up from the boulder warms their backs. Later, they walk down to the riverbank and sit next to the river. Nora rinses her hands off and then cups them together. She dips her cupped hands in the water and brings it up to her mouth. She leans forward and drinks the cool water. Runi eagerly drinks water too.

"Do you want to go home?" Runi asks.

"Not yet! Let's try hunting one more time," Nora replies.

"That's what I'd like to do," says Runi. "I really want another chance to bring back more than just berries for dinner."

Nora and Runi walk to the field near the trees again. This time, Runi moves about eight paces from Nora. In silence, they walk with their spears ready. They stop now and then to survey the area around them. Suddenly, two rabbits dart out from behind a log. One races for a tree and the other jumps toward the back of a tree stump. Runi swiftly throws his spear at the rabbit nearing the tree. The spear hits the rabbit and kills it instantly. Runi stands trembling. Nora shouts, "Food for dinner tonight!"

Runi walks over and looks quietly at the rabbit. He carefully pulls his spear out of the rabbit and lays the rabbit on its side.

"Are you alright?" asks Nora.

"Well, I like eating rabbit, so I am glad for the food, plus my shot looks pretty accurate. But I'm not used to killing a rabbit," replies Runi.

"Actually, your shot was really accurate," Nora says. "It died right away. It's not like you hit it in the leg and it was limping around for hours and we had to chase it. We're just hunting a rabbit that can't hurt us. When we get big enough for the adult hunt, we could be hunting a woolly mammoth."

"I know," says Runi. "I'm getting tired. Let's get ready and go home." He picks up

the rabbit and the children head back to their cave.

As Nora and Runi climb up the mountain toward home, they see several adult hunters carrying a deer to their cave. The children begin hurrying up the hill to join them.

Photo credit: Shannon McPherron, Abri Peyrony Project, License CC-BY-SA 2.0

A lissoir—view from the front, back, and sides

This bone tool was found in a Neanderthal site at Abri Peyrony in France. It is called a lissoir, which means "to make smooth," and was used to scrape animal hides. After animal hides are cleaned and rinsed, they can still be very stiff. Scraping them with a lissoir makes the hides soft and smooth. Then they can be used as blankets or clothes to keep warm in winter.

CHAPTER THREE

NORA AND RUNI ARRIVE AT THE ENTRANCE to their cave just as two of the hunters, Gobi and Murla, are leaning their spears against the wall.

Gobi walks over to the lifeless deer that lies on the ground. He carefully works part of a broken spear out of its chest and tests the tip of the spear. It remains sharp, smooth, and unbroken. He shows it to Murla. She examines it and says, "I think it can be used again." Gobi nods in agreement and puts the broken spear on the ground next to the wall.

Gobi, Murla, and several other hunters lift the animal and carry it to the far side of the cave near the front. They gently lay the animal down. The deer will be skinned immediately. The skin will be set to one side and prepared so it can be used for clothes. Then the meat will be cut up. In a few hours some of the meat will be cooked over a fire and eaten at dinner where everyone will celebrate the successful hunt. Some meat will be prepared so it can be eaten later in the week. Other meat will be dried so it can be eaten even later.

Nora and Runi go over to an area near the firepit. There is a large rock with a flat surface. On top of the rock is a pile of chestnuts. Nora gently takes the berries from her pouch and puts them next to the chestnuts. Runi lays the rabbit on the other side of the rock. Then Nora says goodbye to Runi and goes to find her mom. She sees her mom near the side of the cave and goes up to her. "Guess what, Mom? Runi got a rabbit and he put it near the fire. We can eat some at dinner. Someone also put chestnuts there for tonight."

"That's great," her mom says. "Why don't you come with me and help me get some deer skin ready for this winter? The deer skin we rinsed out at the river a few days ago needs to be softened. I've gotten some of the stiffness out of it, but it needs more work."

"Sure," replies Nora. Nora goes with her mom to get the piece of deer skin that her mom wants to work on. They bring it to the side of the cave and put it on the floor. Nora's mom sits down and puts her lissoir on the floor next to her. The lissoir is a bone tool that Nora's mom uses to make the deer skin waterproof and soft. Nora sits across from her and holds her side of the deer skin while her mom flattens it out. Then her mom puts a rock at the top of the deer skin to hold it in place and picks up her lissoir.

"Now, hold on while I scrape underneath the deer skin," she says to Nora.

"I'm holding it tight," Nora replies. Nora's

mom blows some dust off her lissoir. Then she begins gently scraping the underside of the deer skin. Nora watches her while making sure to hold the deer skin tight.

"Mom, maybe next time, I can help you scrape the deer skin," asks Nora.

Her mom looks at her and replies, "You have to be really careful when you are scraping because you don't want to poke a hole in the deer skin. Once you make a hole, it's permanent. You will be ready for this job in a year or so, and I'll show you how to do it then. I promise."

For the next hour, they work quietly together. Then Nora has an idea. "Mom, do you think we could use some of this deer skin to make a pair of boots for me this winter?" asks Nora.

"Maybe," replies her mom. "What about the ones you wore last winter?"

"I think my feet are too big now," replies Nora. Her mom laughs and says, "When it gets colder, we'll decide what to do."

After they have worked on the deer skin, Nora helps her mom put it on the floor next to the wall of the cave. If there is time tomorrow, they will take the deer skin and work on it again until it is even more supple and smooth. But for today, their task is finished. Nora's mom looks at her and says, "Nora, you were a big help. You can go."

"Thanks, Mom," replies Nora. "I'm going to get ready and then go eat dinner."

Nora doesn't want to miss anything tonight. She knows it will be special and that after everyone has eaten, there will be stories and maybe even singing and dancing to celebrate. She wants to look nice for tonight.

Nora walks back to where she sleeps and finds her pouch where she keeps all the favorite things that she has collected. She looks inside her pouch at the different colored beads, shells, a tiny green stone, and small feathers from different birds. She takes out her feathers and looks at them. She decides not to wear them tonight. She has another idea, so she puts her feathers back. For tonight, she takes out her red-beaded necklace. Red is Nora's favorite color, and her mom helped her make this necklace out of leather string and three red beads. Nora puts the necklace around her neck. She's ready now, and she hurries over to the fire.

Photo credit: Luka Mjeda (2015), Krapina Neanderthal site, License CC-BY-4.0

Eagle claws used for Neanderthal decorations

At a Neanderthal site in Krapina, Croatia, these white-tailed eagle claws were discovered. The claws have been filed and holes have been made in them. They could have been made into a necklace or some other kind of jewelry. This is evidence that Neanderthals made objects to use as decorations. These eagle claw decorations were made 130,000 years ago.

CHAPTER FOUR

PEOPLE ARE GATHERING FOR THE EVENING meal. The deer meat is roasting over the fire. Next to the fire, the rabbit meat is cooked and ready to eat. Nora sees Runi and waves. Runi stops by the fire and picks up a piece of rabbit meat. He tears it in two pieces and walks over to Nora.

"Do you want some?" he asks Nora, offering her a piece.

"Of course," Nora replies as she takes it and pops it in her mouth. "I think tonight is going to be fun."

"Yeah," replies Runi, "they built a huge fire. We'll be up late tonight. Hey, is that a necklace you are wearing?"

"Yes," replies Nora. "My mom helped me make it at the beginning of summer. It's red because that's my favorite color."

"My dad's wearing his necklace tonight," comments Runi. "He calls it his cave bear necklace because it has part of a cave bear tooth on it. The tooth is from the cave bear that attacked my grandpa."

"I've seen his necklace. But there are other things on it too," replies Nora.

"He puts things on it that he likes and that bring good luck. He found a shell once at the river and he put that on it."

"I'm going to go stay near the fire where it's warmer," says Nora.

"I'm going to find my mom and dad. I'll see you later," replies Runi.

Nora's mom sees Nora sitting near the fire. She walks over and sits next to Nora. Her mom is holding some deer meat and chestnuts. "Do you want to share some of this?" she says and smiles at Nora. Then she sees the necklace. "Nice necklace—it looks great on you!"

"Thanks, Mom, and yes, I'm hungry now," replies Nora. Nora takes a piece of deer meat and slowly chews it. It is delicious. Then she bites into a warm chestnut.

"Mmm," Nora says while looking up at her mom. "This is another favorite meal."

"Do you want some berries later?" her mom asks.

"No, thank you, I had plenty this morning," replies Nora. After finishing her food, Nora looks around at all the people now seated near the fire. Everyone is here.

After everyone finishes eating, Gobi stands. He announces, "Today, we can say with pride that our trackers are sharp and able to find animals. Our spear shots are accurate because we train hard and support one another in the chase. We are grateful the deer died quickly, and his death allows us to live. Now, there is food for everyone. You know that this is not always what happens. Many times we have gone to bed hungry. But today was a good hunting day. We give thanks for this. Soon, the nights will turn much colder than tonight. But tonight, the moon is bright and round against a clear sky with many stars shining down on us. It's a good night for a warm fire and a celebration." Then Gobi sits down.

Murla stands and begins to sing a song about hunting. She sings about tracking, ambushing, and taking down deer, cave bears, and woolly mammoths. Slowly, people around the fire begin humming along and clapping. Some people nod their heads and join in. Others stand and begin to sway in place, and others step back from the group and start dancing. Nora joins the dancers in the back. She likes to jump, twirl, and tap her feet to the beat.

She moves to the different rhythms of the songs. Other adults, children, and teenagers join the dancing, including Runi and his mom and dad. Several more people sing songs. Then everyone joins in a popular song, singing it loudly while clapping and dancing. Everyone is laughing and having a great time! Then some people start to get tired and sit down for a rest.

Next, Runi's father tells stories about three different birds. He describes the birds and mimics their calls. He even flaps his arms to show how the birds fly. In one story he follows the hatching of a small bird that is fed by its parents. The chick slowly grows bigger. Everyone laughs at the part of the story where the chick flaps its wings on the edge of the nest each day but is too scared to leave. Finally the chick is big enough and jumps out of the nest and onto the branch and then soars away from the tree. More people share stories and then another couple of songs. Nora joins the dancing whenever there is a song. But finally, she is tired from dancing and goes over to sit next to her mom. She listens and watches. The cave is warm, and Nora loves watching and hearing what everyone has to share.

Nora begins to feel drowsy and leans her head on her mom's shoulder.

"I think it's time for bed," her mom says.

"Oh not yet. I just want to stay and hear one more song and one more story, and then I want to go outside and look at the sky," replies Nora. Her mom moves closer to Nora and puts her arm around her.

"OK," she says, "but after that it's time for bed." Nora nods. She listens for a while and then slowly her eyes close and she becomes still. Her mom leans over and says gently, "Now it's time." Nora nods sleepily. Her mom pulls her up to her feet. The two of them go out past the fire to the front of the cave. Nora stands and looks up at the night sky. The full moon shines, and more than a thousand stars sparkle.

"Mom, it's such a bright sky, it's almost alive." Then Nora shouts, "Hello stars, it's Nora here, saying hello!" Nora starts giggling.

Her mom laughs and says, "Go ahead and shout. It's the end of the warm months and next we get ready for snow. But tonight is for being happy." They continue looking at the night sky shimmering down on them.

Then slowly, they turn around and walk to where their family sleeps. Nora lies down on a pile of animal skins on the floor, and her mom gently pulls a bear skin over her.

"Today is the best day of my life, ever," Nora tells her mom.

"Good night," her mom replies. Nora snuggles in and drifts off to sleep.

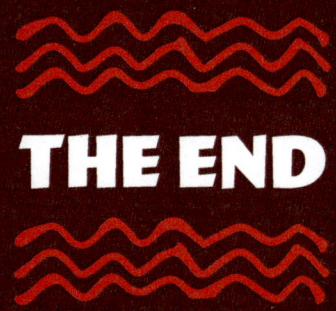

GLOSSARY

anthropologist: a person who studies the origins of humans, such as how we lived in prehistoric times

bone tool: a tool that is created from the bone of an animal. These tools are some of the earliest tools ever made.

cave bear: an extinct bear that lived in caves in Europe and Asia during prehistoric times

extinct: no longer existing. It used to exist but doesn't anymore.

flaked stone tool: a type of tool that is made of stone. The stone is hit so that a piece of the stone falls off. This is done to make the stone sharp like a knife. It can then be used to sand wood or cut food.

hominin: a group that includes modern humans, extinct human species, and all our immediate ancestors

lissoir: a bone tool invented by Neanderthals to soften animal hides

Neanderthals: an extinct species or subspecies of ancient humans

vigilant: keeping careful watch for possible danger or difficulties

woolly mammoth: a very large elephant-like animal that lived during prehistoric times and then went extinct

ACKNOWLEDGMENTS

To the professionals from Reedsy.com, I give a big thank-you for your skills and hard work in bringing this book from its manuscript to its published form. Many thanks to Karina Granda for her cover and interior design and art direction, Isabelle Arné for her illustrations, Alex Messina-Schultheis for her editorial assessment and proofreading, and Tom Klonoski and Kelly Messier for their copyediting.

To my friends and family, thank you for being there as I struggled through numerous revisions of my book. Thank you to Breeda for the zoom discussions, Magloire for sending flowers on Whatsapp, and

Kathleen, Donald, Chris, and Jenny for facetime conversations. A special thanks to my in-person family pod: my niece Rose, who shared her *Times* crossword puzzle every Sunday, and to my brother Tom, who gave me a room in his house to work on my book.

This book wouldn't have happened without the encouragement from all of you during the COVID-19 pandemic. I am deeply grateful for your support.

Mary A. Graves taught social studies to middle and high school students in California, Taiwan, Japan, Togo, and Iraq. While in Iraq, she visited Shanidar Cave, a famous Neanderthal site. She was impressed by the cave and began reading more about Neanderthals. She decided to write about what life might have been like for Neanderthal children. This is that book. She hopes you like it.

Isabelle Arné is a French illustrator. Creating beautiful illustrations for stories is one of her passions. She is the author-illustrator of *Alone*, a book about Fluffy, a cat living in a magical universe. She likes to hike and take care of small plants. She lives in Bordeaux, France. You can stop in and visit her at isabellearne.com.

Made in the USA
Coppell, TX
08 December 2022